OLYMPIC SPORTS

CYCLING

by Clive Gifford

amicus

Published by Amicus
P.O. Box 1329
Mankato, MN 56002

Printed in the United States of America, at Corporate Graphics in North Mankato, Minnesota.

Library of Congress Cataloging-in-Publication Data
Gifford, Clive.
 Cycling / by Clive Gifford.
    p. cm. — (Olympic sports)
 Includes index.
 Summary: "An introduction to a variety of cycling events of the summer Olympics, including road racing, time trials, triathalon, mountain biking, BMX racing, and more. Also explains rules, records, and famous Olympic cyclists"--Provided by publisher.
 ISBN 978-1-60753-190-6 (library bound)
 1. Cycling—Juvenile literature. 2. Olympics—Juvenile literature. I. Title.
 GV1043.5.G54 2012
 796.6--dc22
                            2011004300

Created by Appleseed Editions, Ltd.
Designed by Helen James
Edited by Mary-Jane Wilkins
Picture research by Su Alexander

Picture credits
page 4 AFP/Getty Images; 5t Vias2000/Shutterstock, b David Fowler/Shutterstock; 6 AFP/Getty Images; 7 Marc Pagani Photography/Shutterstock; 8 Getty Images; 9t Chris Curtis/Shutterstock, b Valeria 73/Shutterstock; 10 AFP/Getty Images; 11 Geoffrey Kuchera/Shutterstock; 12 Getty Images; 13 & 14 AFP/Getty Images; 15 Getty Images; 16 AFP/Getty Images; 17 & 18 Getty Images; 19 & 20 AFP/Getty Images; 21 Popperfoto/Getty Images; 22 Getty Images; 23t David Mail/Shutterstock, b AFP/Getty Images; 24, 25 & 26 Getty Images; 27t Timothy Large/Shutterstock, b Getty Images; 28 Getty Images; 29t Getty Images, b Marc Pagani Photography/Shutterstock
Front cover: Getty Images

DAD0051
3-2011

9 8 7 6 5 4 3 2 1

Contents

Going for Gold

The Olympics is international sports competition at its best. Every four years in summer, thousands of athletes, known as Olympians, gather in one city. There, they compete against the best athletes in their sport, hoping to come home with an Olympic gold, silver, or bronze medal.

Germany's Sabine Spitz is delighted to win her first Olympic gold medal. She won a bronze in the mountain bike competition in 2004 and gold at the 2008 games.

MODERN GAMES

The ancient Greek games were held in Olympia from 776 BC for more than a thousand years. In the 1890s, the games were revived when the first modern Olympic games were held in the Greek city of Athens in 1896. Today, the host city and nation welcome tens of thousands of spectators, while millions more watch on television.

DIFFERENT DISCIPLINES

Male cyclists have taken part in the modern Olympics since 1896. Cycling for women was introduced in 1984. The different types of cycling competitions at the games range from track racing events held indoors to long distance road racing events. Some competitions are for individual riders, while others are team events. In more recent years, both mountain biking (see pages 20–23) and BMX racing (see pages 24–27) have been part of the Olympics.

Olympic OoPs

At the 1896 Olympics in Greece, all but two competitors in the 100 kilometer (62.14 mile) road race had withdrawn by the halfway mark. One of the two, Léon Flameng, fell but remounted his bike and became the first ever Olympic cycling gold medalist.

GONE FROM THE GAMES

A number of cycling events were held at some Olympics and have since disappeared. At the 1896 Olympics, there was a 12-hour race that began at 5 A.M. that only two riders finished! Tandems—bicycles ridden by two riders—were first raced at the Olympics in 1908. The last Olympic tandem champions were Vladimir Semenets and Igor Tselovalnykov of the **Soviet Union** in 1972.

FEATS AND RECORDS

At the 1988 Olympics, East Germany's Christa Rothenburger won a silver in the women's sprint cycling, with a silver and gold won in speed skating at the Winter Olympics earlier the same year!

Britain's Jamie Staff displays his 2008 Olympic gold medal for winning the team sprint along with Chris Hoy and Jason Kenny. France received silver, and Germany won bronze.

Road Racing

The first official cycling competition was a 1.2 kilometer (.75 mile) road race through Paris in 1868. Men have competed in a road race at every modern Olympics. The first Olympic road race for women was won by U.S. cyclist Connie Carpenter-Phinney in 1984.

Nicole Cooke roars with delight as she wins gold in the women's road race at the 2008 Olympics. The British rider completed the course in 3 hours, 32 minutes, 24 seconds.

ROAD COURSES

Road races are held on smooth-surfaced roads, but they vary in distance from one games to another. At Beijing in 2008, women raced over 78.5 miles (126.4 km) and men over 152.5 miles (245.4 km). A race begins with all riders massed at the start. Ahead of them is the toughest of competitions in varying weather conditions.

In the 2008 men's race, 53 of the 143 starters dropped out. Samuel Sanchez of Spain won the race in 6 hours, 23 minutes, and 49 seconds.

STREAMLINED RIDERS

Road racing bikes are light, but must weigh at least 14.9 lbs (6.8 kg). Handlebars with brakes and gear levers extend forward so that riders can adopt a **streamlined** position that lets the air move smoothly around them. Cyclists also ride directly behind one another—this can save as much as a quarter of their energy for a powerful sprint to the finish line at the end of the race. Road racers tend to work in groups. The main group of cyclists is known as the **peloton**. At various stages in a race, a lone rider or small group may break away, trying to put crucial distance between themselves and the peloton.

STAGE RACES

Many of the best riders from **professional** road racing teams enter the Olympics. Away from the games, they compete in a wide range of races from short **criterium** events through cities and towns, to races that last for many days and stages. The most prestigious of all stage races are the three Grand Tour competitions, the Giro d'Italia, the Vuelta a España, and the most famous of all, the **Tour de France**. The 2010 Tour de France had 20 stages and covered 2,237 miles (3,600 km) of road.

FEATS AND RECORDS

The 1996 Olympic men's road race lasted almost five hours but had a gripping finish, with the first two riders recording exactly the same time —4 hours, 53 minutes, and 56 seconds. The Swiss rider Pascal Richard beat Rolf Sorensen by less than the width of a wheel.

The leading riders in the 2004 Tour de France enter the final stages of the race in Paris. Lance Armstrong (center) wears the yellow jersey given to the leader. He later won the race.

Time Trial and Triathlon

The Olympic time trial competition is a race **against the clock**. Only men competed in this race between 1912 and 1932, and then it wasn't held until 1996. Since then, both men and women have competed. Each competitor has one attempt to complete the course as fast as they can.

Kristin Armstrong checks the road behind her while completing her time trial at the 2008 games. The American rider won the gold medal.

ROAD TIME TRIAL COURSES

The first time trial in 1912 was a marathon in which cyclists had to cover a huge 196 mile (315.4 km) course—almost the distance from New York to Washington, D.C. Today it is held over a much shorter course than the Olympic road race. At the 2008 Olympics, the time trial was just over 29 miles (47 km) for men and 14 miles (23 km) for women.

STAGGERED START

About 40 men and 25 women compete in the time trial. Each is held in position on the bike by an official, and the riders start the race at 90 second intervals. When the top time trialists are riding, they sometimes overtake the rider ahead of them. Their speed over courses is impressive. The women's 2008 gold medalist, American Kristin Armstrong, averaged 25.131 mph (40.445 km/h).

Olympic OoPs

At the 1920 Olympics in Antwerp, Belgium, the time trial course was 109 miles (175 km) long and included six railway crossings. Harry Stenqvist, the eventual winner, had to wait four minutes for one train to pass before he could go on his way.

Triathletes compete in a long distance triathlon called an Ironman. Competitors swim 2.4 miles (3.86 km), race 112 miles (180.25 km) on bikes, and finally run 26.2 miles (42.2 km).

THE TRIATHLON

Cycling road races are part of one other Olympic medal sport, the **triathlon**. In this endurance event, about 50 competitors cycle in separate races for men and women. They start by swimming 1,500 meters (0.93 miles), then cycle 40 kilometers (24.9 miles), and end with a 10 kilometer (6.2 mile) run. This test of strength and **stamina** was first held at the 2000 Sydney Olympics and has been a hit with spectators.

Superstar

At the 2008 Olympics, Fabian Cancellara from Switzerland passed his rival for the gold medal, Stefan Schumacher, during the time trials. He completed the Beijing course in 1 hour, 2 minutes, and 11 seconds—33 seconds ahead of the runner up.

A competitor in the Cusio Cup triathlon in Italy runs his bike into the transition area before entering the final stage of the triathlon, the 10 km (6.2 mile) run.

On Track

Most Olympic cycling medals are won in track races. These were held outside on a smooth oval riding surface until 1976. Olympic cycling tracks are now always inside a building called a **velodrome**.

Argentina's Juan Esteban Curuchet races behind Marco Arriagada of Chile in the men's points race at the 2008 Olympics. Their track bikes have no brakes or gears.

INSIDE THE VELODROME

An Olympic cycling track is 250 meters (273.4 yds) long and made of smooth wood. It has steeply sloped turns that allow riders to keep up speed around turns. The 2012 Olympic velodrome in Stratford, London seats 6,000 spectators and has underground heating to help thin the air and help cyclists reach their fastest speeds.

CHANGING COMPETITIONS

Not all track cycling events are held at every Olympics. At the 2004 games, the 12 races included a 500 meter (2 laps of the track) time trial for women, as well as a 1,000 meter time trial for men. There were no time trials at the 2008 games. Ten cycling events were held, seven for men and three for women.

THE MADISON

The Madison is a men's event that was held at the 2000, 2004, and 2008 Olympics, but will not be held in 2012. It is 50 kilometers (31 miles) long and involves 18 teams, each with two riders. Only one rider per team races at a time. The other circles the top of the track, waiting to take over for his partner. The goal is to pull ahead of rival teams by whole laps, because the team that completes the most laps wins. Every 20 laps, there is a short sprint after which the fastest four riders gain points. These help to separate teams who finish the race after completing the same number of laps.

EQUAL OPPORTUNITIES

There will be no individual pursuit and points races at the 2012 Olympics. For the first time, men and women will compete in five races each. There were 35 female track cyclists at the 2008 Olympics. That number could rise to 84 in 2012.

Teammates in a Madison race swap positions by using a hand-sling. This helps to push one rider forward faster into the next stage of the race.

Individual Sprint

Men have competed in the individual sprint race at more Olympic games than any other track event, having been left out of only the 1904 and 1912 games. The women's sprint was first held in 1988. Riders often begin slowly and use clever tactics as they **accelerate** to a power-packed, explosive finish.

Britain's Victoria Pendleton moves out to overtake Dutch rider Willy Kanis during the women's sprint race in Beijing.

Superstar

In the 200m qualifying time trial in the 2008 Olympic women's sprint, Britain's Victoria Pendleton set a new Olympic record of 10.963 seconds, an average speed of 40.809 mph (65.675 km/h). She went on to win the gold medal to add to five world championship sprint titles.

COMPLICATED SYSTEM

The individual sprint has the most complicated qualifying system of any track cycling race. First, the riders take part in a 200 meter (219 yard) time trial. They build up speed over two warm-up laps before aiming for their top speed over the last 200 meters. The fastest riders move on to the next rounds, which are races between just two cyclists. The winners of these move onto the next round. The losers enter a parallel competition called the **repechage**. The two or three most successful riders in the repechage then re-enter the main competition for medals.

KNOCK-OUT STAGES

In the sprint competition, pairs of sprinters compete against each other over three races. The first to win two races progresses to the next stage. Cyclists race from a standing start over three or four laps of the velodrome track. The first across the line is the winner.

TRACK TACTICS

Tactics are important in sprint races. Over the first laps, the cyclists may pedal relatively slowly, each making sure they know the position of their opponent. They may perform a track stand—coming to a standstill resting on their pedals—to force an opponent to ride ahead of them.

Riders may also sprint ahead, or move up the steep banks of the track to try to swoop down and attack the position of an opponent.

No track bicycles have gears, so the racers have to rely on great strength, fitness, and leg power to crank up the speed as they accelerate to over 44 mph (70 km/h) in the final sprint for the line.

Germany's Maximilian Levy (right) and Mickael Bourgain of France compete for the bronze medal in the 2008 Olympic men's sprint. Bourgain won two out of three races and took the medal.

Team Sprints and the Keirin

There are two other cycling sprint events for men and women at the Olympics—an individual sprinting race called the keirin and a team sprinting competition.

A Japanese Race

The keirin race was first held in Japan in the 1940s, and keirin racing is now a major sport there. In 2009, a top Japanese rider, Keita Ebine, won more than two million dollars in prize money. This race was held for the first time at the 2000 Olympics. In the final, six cyclists follow a motorized bike called a **derny** for five and a half laps of an eight lap race. The derny gradually speeds up to 31 mph (50 km/h) before leaving the track. The riders then compete in a powerful two-and-a-half lap sprint to the line.

Team Sprint

The first men's team sprint was held at the 2000 Olympics, and it is now one of the most exciting

A motorcycle derny leads a pack of keirin riders at the 2009 UCI world championship. The derny gradually speeds up the pace before leaving the track.

track cycling events. Teams of three riders power along the track in single file so they stay as streamlined as possible. Once the front rider enters a 30 meter long (98 ft.) zone at the end of the first lap, he peels off by moving up the track bank to allow the riders behind to continue racing. Just before the start of the crucial third and final lap, the second rider peels away, leaving one last rider to sprint around the last lap alone.

SHORT SHARP RACES

Team sprint races are held over three laps and last just 45 seconds or so, but demand enormous power and speed. The first women's competition will be held at the 2012 Olympics and will be even shorter, with teams of two cyclists racing over just two laps of the track.

All sprint teams start out by competing in a three lap time trial on their own against the clock. The fastest eight teams enter the heats where they race against another team, with each team starting on opposite sides of the track. The four heat winners compete for medals in two more races.

The British trio of Chris Hoy, Jason Kenny, and Jamie Staff race in the team sprint event at the 2008 Olympics, where they won gold.

Pursuits and Points Races

Two popular track cycling races are pursuits and points races. At the Olympics, there are both team and individual pursuits. Team pursuit races tend to be crowded endurance events.

The New Zealand men's pursuit team tries to overtake their rivals from Spain during the 2008 Olympics.

reports often split the screen to show both lines so viewers can see which rider is ahead in each lap. The winner is the rider who finishes first, but if one rider catches up with the other, that rider wins without riding the rest of the distance.

INDIVIDUAL PURSUIT

This race pits two riders against each other. In the individual pursuit, men race over 4,000 meters (2.5 miles) and women over 3,000 meters (1.86 miles). Both straight sections of the track have a starting or finishing line. Each rider starts the race from one of these lines, and TV

TEAM PURSUIT

The team pursuit event was part of the first London Olympics in 1908. In the men's race, teams of four riders cycle 16 laps of the track. In the women's race, three riders cycle 12 laps. All the team members start off at the same time, and they cut down on **wind resistance** by riding behind one another. Riders move in and out of the front position to save energy. A team's time is recorded as the moment the front wheel of the team's last rider reaches the finish line.

POINTS PACES

These crowded track races demand great endurance. Men race over 40 kilometers (24.85 miles) and women over 25 kilometers (15.53 miles). They need to be constantly aware of the progress of the race and also need great sprinting power, as a sprint is held after every ten laps. Points are awarded to the first four finishers (five points for the winner, then three, two, and one).

FEATS AND RECORDS

Great Britain won the first team pursuit competition in 1908, but waited exactly 100 years before winning it again. The winning team included Bradley Wiggins, who also won the 2004 and the 2008 individual pursuit.

POINTS TACTICS

Some riders save energy for the sprints. Others power ahead, trying to get a full lap ahead of their opponents. If they succeed, they win 20 points and then defend their lead. The rider with the most points at the end wins. At the 2008 Olympics, Spain's Joan Llaneras gained two laps on the rest of the field, as well as 20 points in the sprints. His total of 60 won him the gold medal. In the women's race, Marianne Vos of the Netherlands earned 10 sprinting points and won by being the only rider to go a lap ahead.

Great Britain's Bradley Wiggins crosses the finish line in the 2008 men's individual pursuit. He beat New Zealand's Hayden Roulston by more than 2.5 seconds to win gold in the event for a second time.

The Omnium

A brand new Olympic event will test the all-round abilities of 24 men and women track cyclists at the London Olympics in 2012. The omnium will include six different races, with the points scored in each counting toward the overall title.

Ed Clancy of Great Britain takes part in the Omnium at the 2010 UCI track cycling world championships in Denmark. Clancy won gold in the team pursuit at the 2008 Olympics.

How Many Events?

Omniums often include five events, but the 2012 Olympic omnium will have six, held over two days. Each country can enter just one rider in the men's and one in the women's competition. The events for men include short time trial sprints, a 30 kilometer (18.64 mile) points race, and a 4 kilometer (2.5 mile) individual and 500 meters for women. The second event is a flying lap in which the cyclists build up speed on the track and are then timed over a single lap ridden at breakneck speed.

ELIMINATION RACE

The last event in the Olympic omnium is a race for all 24 riders. It is called an elimination race, and is also known as devil take the hindmost, or miss and out. In this exciting event, the riders try to stay with the pack and not fall behind. Every two laps, the last rider is eliminated and has to leave the race. As the numbers thin out, the tension mounts until just two riders are left to compete over the final two laps.

pursuit race. Women will compete in time trial sprints, a 20 kilometer (12.4 mile) points race, and a 3 kilometer (1.9 mile) individual pursuit.

FEWEST POINTS WINS

Riders are awarded points for each event, depending on the rider's finishing position. The last rider receives 24 points and the winning rider just one point. The points are added up over the six events. The winner is the cyclist with the fewest points.

TIME TRIALS

Two of the Olympic omnium's six events are time trials in which officials time the cyclist to see who rides fastest. The regular time trial will be 1,000 meters long for men

A crowded pack competes in the points race of the women's Omnium at the 2009 UCI track cycling world championships. The race was won by Josephine Tomic of Australia.

Mountain Biking

Mountain biking is the fastest growing cycling sport in the world, with thousands of new riders taking part in local competitions. It arrived at the Olympics in 1996, when separate cross-country races were held for men and women.

Mountain bikers Liam Killeen and Yamamoto Kohei face a steep drop on the Beijing Olympic cross-country course. Riders have to stay balanced and keep up their speed throughout the race.

CROSS-COUNTRY RACING

Cross-country mountain bike races are held on a marked off-road course. All competitors start the race at the same time and cycle over a number of laps of the course. Races are 25–31 miles (40–50 km) long for men and 19–25 miles (30–40 km) for women. The first rider across the finish line is the winner.

LAPPED

During a race, any rider who is lapped (overtaken) by the race leader completes the lap they are on before leaving the race. In the 2008 Olympics men's race on the 2.9 mile (4.6 km) long Laoshan mountain bike course, 20 riders were lapped and did not complete the race.

COURSE CHALLENGES

Every cross-country course is different, but they all share similar features and present similar challenges to riders. The course runs over different types of ground, including rocky trails, dirt tracks, gravel paths, and forest roads. No more than 15 percent of the course can be on smooth roads, and the courses also have plenty of sharp dips and drops on steep **gradients**, as well as lung-bursting climbs.

Superstar

Olympic mountain bike races last around two hours, although the medal winners tend to finish earlier. At the 2008 games, the women's gold medalist, Sabine Spitz of Germany, completed the six laps in 1 hour 45:11 minutes.

Pro Bikes

The bikes used by top riders in major competitions, such as the Olympics, are advanced versions of regular mountain bikes. They have powerful disc brakes and tough but light frames made from materials such as carbon fiber and titanium **alloys**. The bikes weigh between 15–24 lbs (7–11 kg). Unlike other bikes at the Olympics, the front wheel forks have a suspension to help soften some of the bumps and dips in the ground.

The men's cross-country race at the 2000 Olympics in Sydney begins with a massed start by 49 cyclists. The race was won by France's Miguel Martinez in 2 hours, 9 minutes, and 2 seconds.

FEATS AND RECORDS

Italian mountain biker Paola Pezzo fell at a hairpin turn in 1996. She got back up and by the 11 km (7 mile) of the 31.9 km (19.8 mile) race, she took the lead. She won by 67 seconds, and in 2000 won again to become mountain biking's first double gold medalist.

RACE SET-UP

Riders can inspect, and sometimes test ride, the course before a race and may make adjustments to their bikes. They can choose their own precise gearing. Many top riders race bikes with 27 gears. Tires are wide and have a rough, knobby **tread** to grip the ground without slowing down the bike too much.

FACING OBSTACLES

Olympic mountain biking is a severe test of a racing cylist's handling skills, as well as of fitness and stamina. Two hours of flat-out racing is physically draining, so riders can take energy drinks at feeding stations dotted around the course. Tree branches or trunks, ruts, boulders, and sometimes water-filled ditches challenge the riders, who perform **bunny hops** or **wheelies** to leap over smaller obstacles, as well as take corners sharply at a steep angle.

CROSS-COUNTRY CHAMPIONS

The cyclists who start each Olympic mountain bike race come from all over the world, but European riders have dominated previous races. In the men's 2008 event, for example,

A mountain biker performs a wheelie, raising his front wheel off the ground to clear an obstacle. Bikers have to clear with jumps and land safely, while trying to lose as little speed as possible.

Daniel McConnell of Australia races down a slope on the 2008 Olympic mountain biking course. Competitors need to steer around and over boulders, ruts, and dips.

Superstar

The first man to win two Olympic mountain biking gold medals was Julien Absalon. The French rider won the event at both the 2004 and 2008 games.

the first non-European finisher was South African Burry Stander, who came in fifteenth.

OTHER MOUNTAIN BIKING EVENTS

Away from the Olympics, there are other mountain bike events besides cross-country races. Downhill racing involves a steep descent on which riders race one at a time against the clock, testing their nerves as they hurtle down scarily steep slopes. Four cross (or 4X) is similar, but pits four riders against each other at the same time. A 4X competition has knock-out rounds in which winning riders progress through the races to reach the final.

BMX Racing

Competitors in the Olympics' newest cycle sport raced in Beijing in 2008. Bicycle motocross, or BMX racing, is fast, frantic, and exciting as eight riders per race speed over a course full of dips, bumps, and turns.

BMX riders fly over bumps during a heat of the women's BMX race in Beijing. BMX racing attracts large crowds because of its bursts of exciting action.

BMX BEGINNINGS
BMX racing began in California in the late 1960s. The sport became hugely popular and was added to the 2008 Olympics. The men's and women's time trial cycling events were removed to create space for the BMX events.

SMALL TOUGH BIKES
BMX bikes are the smallest bicycles in cycle racing. The bikes' compact frames are light but tough. The wheels are 20 inches (51 cm) in diameter and have wide tires with a chunky, knobby tread for good grip on the dirt track. Bikes have a single gear and only one brake, which works on the back wheel. Riders wear protective racing suits with padding and full face helmets since crashes and falls are common.

RACING COURSES
A BMX course is around 383 yards (350 m) long. It is designed and built to challenge riders and test their bravery, skill, and strength, as well as

allow for exciting, high-speed racing on straights and large banked turns called **berms**. Obstacles range from small bumps and sudden dips to large ramp-like slopes that allow racers to jump and fly up to 33 feet (10 m) through the air.

RAPID RACING

Every BMX race at the Olympics takes around 40 seconds to complete. Riders have no gear changes to help them build speed. Instead, they pump their legs vigorously to build speed, and they try to brake as little as possible to maintain a high speed that they can still control. Racers can reach 34–37 mph (55–60 km/h) on downhill stretches of the course.

Māris Štrombergs wins Latvia's only gold medal of the 2008 Olympics in the men's BMX. Štrombergs won all three races in the semi-final and won the final with a time of 36.19 seconds.

Britain's Shanaze Reade (left) flies over a hump during the three-race semi finals to decide who would qualify for the women's BMX final in 2008.

QUALIFYING TO RACE

An Olympic BMX competition involves 32 men and 16 women. They qualify for the games with their performances in previous competitions run by the International Cycling Union (UCI). Up to three men and two women from any one country can compete at the games.

The Olympic competition begins with two attempts at a single lap time trial. Their fastest lap counts toward their seeding (placement) as all riders enter the heats.

HEATS AND FINAL

Riders are divided into groups of eight, and take part in three races called heats. They are awarded points based on their finishing position in each heat to decide which four racers go on to the next round. The final is a single, winner-takes-all race between the eight best riders.

FAST START

Each race begins with the eight riders in a line in front of a horizontal barrier called the start gate

BMX racers lean into the tight turns of the course, pedalling hard, but trying to steer a fast, steady line through the corner.

at the top of a slope. Traffic lights and beeping sounds signal a countdown, and as the gate drops, the riders strain every muscle to make an explosive start out of the gate. Their goal is to get a good holeshot, which means to be in the lead by the time they reach the first turn.

TURNS AND JUMPS

The races are intense, as all the riders are looking for small gaps in the field or good racing positions when going into turns that will allow them to overtake rivals. As they race, they have to deal with a challenging series of different-sized jumps. Riders try to wheelie over the smallest obstacles, while keeping the bike's back wheel on the ground. This transmits power and moves them forward. On larger jumps, riders try for a fast, flat flight path through the air so they land back on the ground as soon as possible.

EXPENSIVE TRAINING

The U.S. BMX Olympic Committee and U.S.A. Cycling built a replica of the Beijing Olympic BMX course in Chula Vista, California for their cyclists to use for training. It cost around $1 million to build.

Olympic hopefuls compete in the 2008 U.S. BMX trials at a course in California. The leader in this race, Mike Day, won the trials and competed at the 2008 games where he won a silver medal.

Gold Medal Greats

Some cyclists rise above their rivals to become legends in their sport. Here are profiles of four of the most famous to take part in the Olympics.

of all time. To add to his outstanding Olympic performances, Hoy also boasts an incredible ten world championship gold medals.

Chris Hoy celebrates winning an Olympic gold in the men's sprint finals at Beijing's Laoshan Velodrome in 2008.

JEANNIE LONGO

France's Jeannie Longo is the most successful women's cyclist of all time, with an amazing 13 world championship titles in road racing and time trials. She has competed at every Olympics since women's cycling events were first held in 1984. Bad luck and injury restricted her chances, but she won a gold medal in 1996, silver medals in 1992 and 1996, and a bronze in 2000. In 2008, at the age of 49, she won her fifteenth French road race championship and qualified for her seventh Olympics in a row, a staggering feat.

CHRIS HOY

Chris Hoy became the first British competitor in 100 years to win three gold medals at the same Olympics—in 2008 his victories in the sprint, team sprint, and keirin events in Beijing set the record. Hoy had won a gold in the kilo time trial race at Athens in 2004 and a silver in the team sprint in 2000. This medal collection makes him the most successful Olympic track cyclist

FEATS AND RECORDS
Jeannie Longo is mainly a road racer, but she has won ten UCI world championship medals in track racing and a silver medal in the world mountain biking championships in 1993.

Olympic OoPs

Leontien van Moorsel entered the 2004 Olympics road race as the favorite, but crashed on the penultimate lap. Despite injuries, she took part in the time trial a few days later and won by more than 24 seconds.

he was diagnosed with cancer, which spread from his testicles to his lungs and brain. He recovered and re-entered competitive cycling, beating his rivals to win an amazing seven Tour de France victories in a row, as well as a bronze medal in the time trial at the 2000 Olympics. He retired after his seventh Tour de France win in 2005, but made a comeback four years later, finishing third in the 2009 Tour de France.

Lance Armstrong powers through the time trials of the 2004 Tour de France on his way to a sixth victory. His winning time was 6 minutes and 19 seconds ahead of second place.

LEONTIEN VAN MOORSEL

The Netherland's greatest ever Olympic cyclist, Leontien van Moorsel, won two world championship gold medals in 1990 and was one of the leading cyclists of the decade. At the 2000 Olympics, she won both the road race and time trial. She then headed onto the track to win a third gold medal in the three kilometer (1.9 mile) pursuit race and a silver medal in the points race. She added a gold and bronze at the 2004 Olympics to hold more Olympic medals than any other cyclist.

LANCE ARMSTRONG

Armstrong was a successful triathlete as a teenager and then switched to cycling. At his first Olympics in 1992, he finished fourteenth in the road race, which secured him a place on his first professional cycling team. In 1996, Armstrong was given only a 50-50 chance of survival after

Glossary

accelerate   to increase speed

against the clock   the term for a race or event in which a rider is timed over a set length course, rather than competing against other riders

alloy   a mixture of metals used to make a light, but strong bike

berm   a bank on a BMX course built on the outside of a turn to create a curve

bunny hop   lifting both wheels of a mountain bike off the ground at the same time, usually to clear an obstacle

criterium   a road race usually through the streets of a town or city that have been closed to road traffic

derny   a motorized bike used in keirin races to pace racing cyclists

gradient   the steepness of a slope in road racing or mountain biking

International Cycling Union (UCI)   The *Union Cycliste Internationale* is the organization that runs world cycling.

peloton   the main group of riders in road racing

professional   a team member who is paid and makes a living from competing in cycling competitions

repechage   a round of racing in a track competition where losers of previous heats race against each other to re-enter the main competition

Soviet Union   the country made up of Russia, Ukraine, and other republics that existed between 1922 and 1991 and competed in the Olympics between 1952 and 1988

stamina   the ability of an athlete's body to perform at peak levels for long periods of time

streamline   to create as smooth a shape as possible so that air flows easily around cyclists and slows them down as little as possible

time trial   a race in which either an individual or team rides over a specific distance against the clock

Tour de France   an annual cycling race, mostly through France, in which the world's top road cycling teams compete

tread   the pattern on a tire's surface that touches the ground or track

triathlon   an Olympic endurance event in which competitors swim, bike, and run; the first to complete the course is the winner.

velodrome   a smooth-surfaced cycle racing track with banked corners

wheelie   to lift the front wheel of the bike off the ground to clear an obstacle in BMX and mountain biking

wind resistance   the force of air pushing against cyclists and slowing them down as they move through the air

Books

Cycling by Paul Mason (Sea-to-Sea Publications, 2010)

Cycling Science by James Bow (Crabtree Pub. Co., 2009)

Extreme Mountain Biking by Daniel Benjamin (Marshall Cavendish Benchmark, 2012)

Lance Armstrong: Racing Hero by Peter Hicks (PowerKids Press, 2011)

The Olympics: Records by Moira Butterfield (Sea-to-Sea Publications, 2012)

Web Sites

http://www.uci.ch/
The web site of the International Cycling Union has information on major competitions.

http://www.olympic.org/
The web site of the International Olympic Committee (IOC). Click on sports links, and select cycling for news, details, and history of cycling sports at the games.

http://www.cyclingnews.com/
Results and news of races and riders in competitions all over the world.

http://www.usacycling.org/
The U.S. cycling team's web pages with lots of information on cycle racing.

http://letour.fr
The official web site of the Tour de France.

http://www.lancearmstrong.com
Learn more about Lance Armstrong's remarkable cycling career.

Index